You...

Emma Dodd

templar

I love **every** bit of you,
your eyes and ears and nose.

I love every bit of you,
from your head down
to your toes.

I love your tumbles,
jumps and bumps,
your fidgets
and your wriggles.

I love your smile,
I love your frown,
your whispers
and your giggles.

I love your games
of hide and seek...

your messes and
your muddles.

I love your bedtime
best of all –
its kisses and its cuddles.

I love you when you're having fun...

and when you're sometimes sad.

I love you when you're kind and good...

and even when you're bad.

Yes, I love **every** bit of you,
and this I know for sure...

with every day
that passes by...

I love you more

nd **more!**

A TEMPLAR BOOK

First published in the UK in 2010 by Templar Publishing
This softback edition published in 2013 by Templar Publishing,
an imprint of The Templar Company Limited,
Deepdene Lodge, Deepdene Avenue, Dorking, Surrey, RH5 4AT
www.templarco.co.uk

Copyright © 2010 by Emma Dodd

1 3 5 7 9 10 8 6 4 2

ISBN: 978-1-84877-651-7

Printed in China